Two for One

BiNK & gollie

Two for One

Kate DiCamillo and Alison McGhee

illustrated by Tony Fucile

WALKER
BOOKS

For Janie, a blue-ribbon friend

K. D.

To Caroly Bintz

A. M.

To Elinor and Eli, great buddies of mine

T. F.

First published 2012 by Walker Books Ltd
87 Vauxhall Walk, London SE11 5HJ

2 4 6 8 10 9 7 5 3 1

Text © 2012 Kate DiCamillo and Alison McGhee
Illustrations © 2012 Tony Fucile

The right of Kate DiCamillo, Alison McGhee and Tony Fucile to be identified as
authors and illustrator respectively of this work has been asserted by them
in accordance with the Copyright, Designs and Patents Act 1988

This book has been typeset in Humana Sans

Printed in China

British Library Cataloguing in Publication Data:
a catalogue record for this book is available from the British Library

ISBN 978-1-4063-3739-6

www.walker.co.uk

Contents

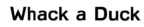

"Gollie, do you think we should go to the spring fair?"

Whack

a

Duck

"Step right up," said the duck man. "Whack a duck!"

"I'm going to win the world's largest doughnut,"

said Bink.

"Of course you are, little lady," said the Whack-a-Duck man. "You've got *winner* written all over you."

"I have?" said Bink.

"She has?" said Gollie.

"What a happy, happy day," said the duck man. "How I love it when little ladies win large doughnuts."

"She hasn't won it yet," said Gollie.

"Who doesn't love a doughnut?" said the duck man. "Who doesn't love a large doughnut? Doughnuts are nature's most perfect food."

"They are?" said Gollie.

"Did I win?" said Bink.

"I don't think so," said Gollie.

"Step right up," said the duck man.
"Whack a doughnut! Win a duck."

"Uh-oh," said Gollie.

"Did I win?" said Bink.

"Whack something?" said the duck man.
"Win something?"

"I fear this can only end in tragedy," said Gollie.

"Did I win?" said Bink.

"Oh, Bink," said Gollie. "There are no winners here."

"Don't worry, Bink," said Gollie. "I'm sure the
Whack-a-Duck man will be fine."

"But I've never seen a grown-up cry before,"
said Bink.

"Three bags of doughnuts,
please," said Bink.

23

"I didn't win," said Bink.

"But we're all still alive," said Gollie.

"Duck a whack," said the duck man. "Step right up."

You're
Special,
Aren't
You?

"Oh, Bink," said Gollie. "How I would
love to be in a talent show."

"But you have to stand on a stage," said Bink.

"I can do that," said Gollie.

"But you have to stand on a stage in front of an audience," said Bink.

"I can do that," said Gollie.

"All righty, then," said Bink.

"Excuse me," said Gollie. "Are you in charge of the talent show?"

"Do you have a talent?" said the judge.

"I do," said Gollie. "In fact, I have several."

"That there is a top-quality talent," said the judge.

"Uh-oh," said Bink.

"Timber!" said the judge.

"I can't even guess," said the judge.

"That's my friend," said Bink.

"What's her talent?" said the judge.

"She has several," said Bink.

"What did you say her talent was again?" said the judge.

"Here it comes," said Bink. "Here comes Gollie's talent."

"You call that talent?" said the judge.

"Gollie!" said Bink.

"Gollie," said Bink, "were you afraid up there?"

"Yes," said Gollie.

"What was your talent?" said Bink.

"I was going to recite a poem," said Gollie.
"On stage. In front of an audience."

"These cows are listening," said Bink.
"And so am I."

" 'Old MacDonald'," began Gollie.

"Oh!" said Bink. "I know that one!"

" 'Had a farm,' " said Gollie. " 'E, I...' "

"'E, I...'" said Bink.

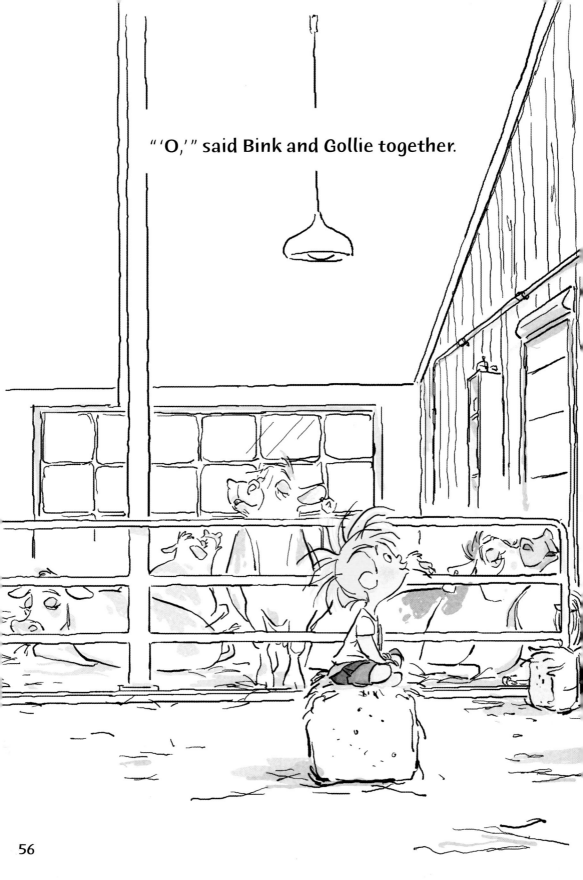

"'O,'" said Bink and Gollie together.

Without
Question

"I love my chipmunk balloon," said Bink.

"I love my sceptre and crown," said Gollie.

"What's next?" said Bink. "The Ferris wheel? The Big Daddy Octopus? The Bump-a-Rama bumper cars?"

"Destiny," said Gollie.

"Destiny?" said Bink. "Is it a ride?"

"In a manner of speaking," said Gollie.

"Girls," said Madame Prunely, "come inside."

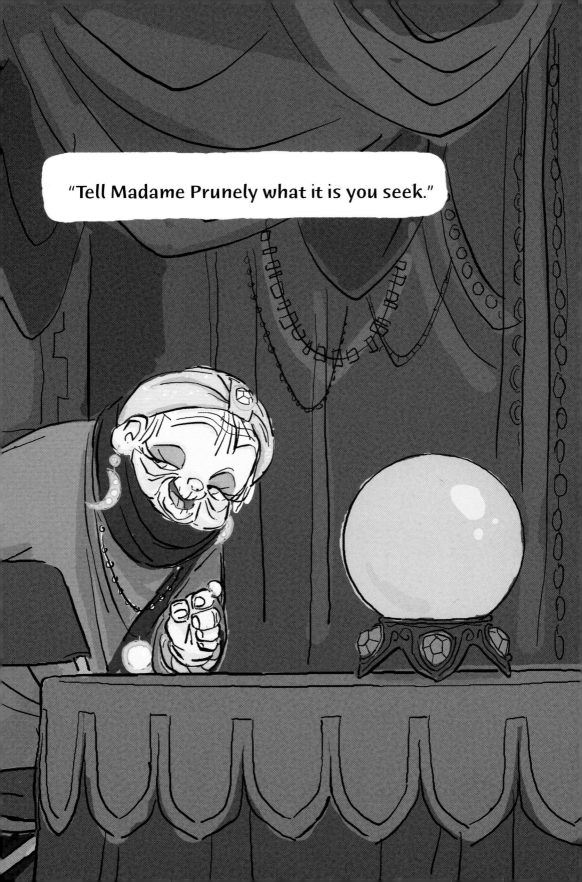

"I gaze into my crystal ball," said Madame Prunely.

"Can I look, too?" said Bink.

"I gaze into my crystal ball," said Madame Prunely. "And I see that the past is replete with loss. A doughnut. A duck. Talent without applause."

"She's right, Gollie," said Bink. "There was a doughnut. There was a duck."

"And no one clapped for me," said Gollie.

"Talk about a darkened path," said Bink.

"But enough about the past," said Madame
Prunely. "Let us take a look at the future."

"I see two friends," said Madame Prunely.

"Is one of those friends tall?" said Gollie.

"Yes," said Madame Prunely.

"And is the other friend short?" said Bink.

"Yes," said Madame Prunely.

"Are they together?" said Gollie.

"Without question," said Madame Prunely.

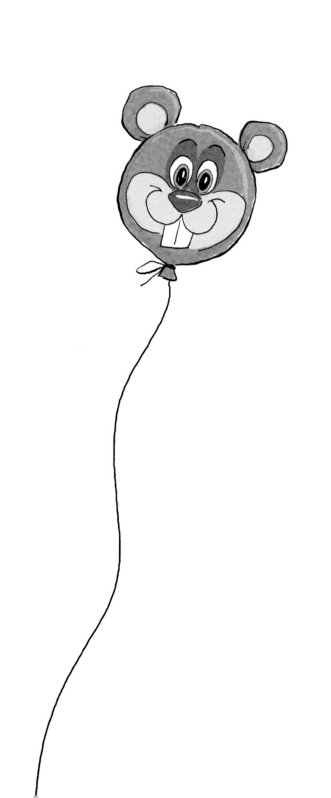

About the creators

Kate DiCamillo is the author of the bestselling *The Magician's Elephant* and the multiple award-winners *The Tale of Despereaux* and *Because of Winn-Dixie*, and the creator of the award-winning Mercy Watson series. Kate DiCamillo lives in Minneapolis, USA.

Alison McGhee is the author of *Song of Middle C*; *Snap*; the young adult novel *All Rivers Flow to the Sea*; and the number 1 bestselling picture book *Someday*. She is also the author of several adult novels, including the bestseller *Shadow Baby*. Alison McGhee lives in Minnesota, USA.

Tony Fucile has spent more than twenty years designing and animating characters for cartoon feature films, including *The Lion King*, *Finding Nemo* and *The Incredibles*, for which he was a supervising animator. His other picture-book titles include *Let's Do Nothing!* and *Driving to Bed*. Tony Fucile lives in San Francisco, USA.

Find out more about *Bink & Gollie* and its creators at
www.binkandgollie.com

Praise for *Bink & Gollie*

A World Book Day "Recommended Read" for 2011

• • •

★ "An exceptional book for early readers"
> — Sarah Webb, *Irish Independent*

★ "With deliciously spare text and delightful cartoons …
wonderfully entertaining."
> — *Lovereading4kids.co.uk*

★ "You'd have to have a heart of stone not to be hypnotized
by the sheer charm of these stories."
> — *School Library Journal*

★ "Oh happiness! Move over Pippi Longstocking! … Bink
and Gollie … celebrate the challenges and strengths of
a great friendship"
> — *New York Times Book Review*

★ "effervescent and endearingly quirky"
> — *Wall Street Journal*

★ "Think Pippi Longstocking meets The Big Bang Theory"
> — *Publishers Weekly*

Available from all good booksellers

www.walker.co.uk